The Wishflower Princess

Kathie Kalafatis

To order additional copies of this book, contact:
Xlibris
1-888-795-4274
www.Xlibris.com
Orders@Xlibris.com

ISBN: Softcover   978-1-7960-8047-6
       Hardcover   978-1-7960-8048-3
       EBook   978-1-7960-8046-9

Library of Congress Control Number: 2019921250

Print information available on the last page

Rev. date: 02/19/2020

In a snow covered castle in a distant land the Wishflower Princess was crying again.

Princess Alexa had lost her 3rd wish, as she sneezed in the air; it went out with a swish.

The princess cried, "This can't happen again, oh whatever would they say, a Wishflower Princess who gives wishes away!"

But as hard as she tried there was nothing she could do. Once they tickled her nose what followed was Ah-Choo!

So she called on her subjects to find her a cure. A bold knight named Sir Chris said, "I'll find one I'm sure."

Then off he went on his trusty old steed, a tortoise named Boris to aid his good deed. He came upon a fair maiden all covered in lace, who sang a sad song as tears fell from her face.

"My dear lady," said Chris. "What has made you so sad? A pretty maiden like you should be happy and glad."

Lady Kayla looked up with the saddest of eyes,
"You must understand there've been terrible lies.
I've lost all hope that our kingdom can recover
from the evil spells that were cast by my mother."

She has taken away all the hope in the world by casting a spell on the wishflower girl." Lady Kayla told the story of why she felt sad and explained how her mother had truly felt bad.

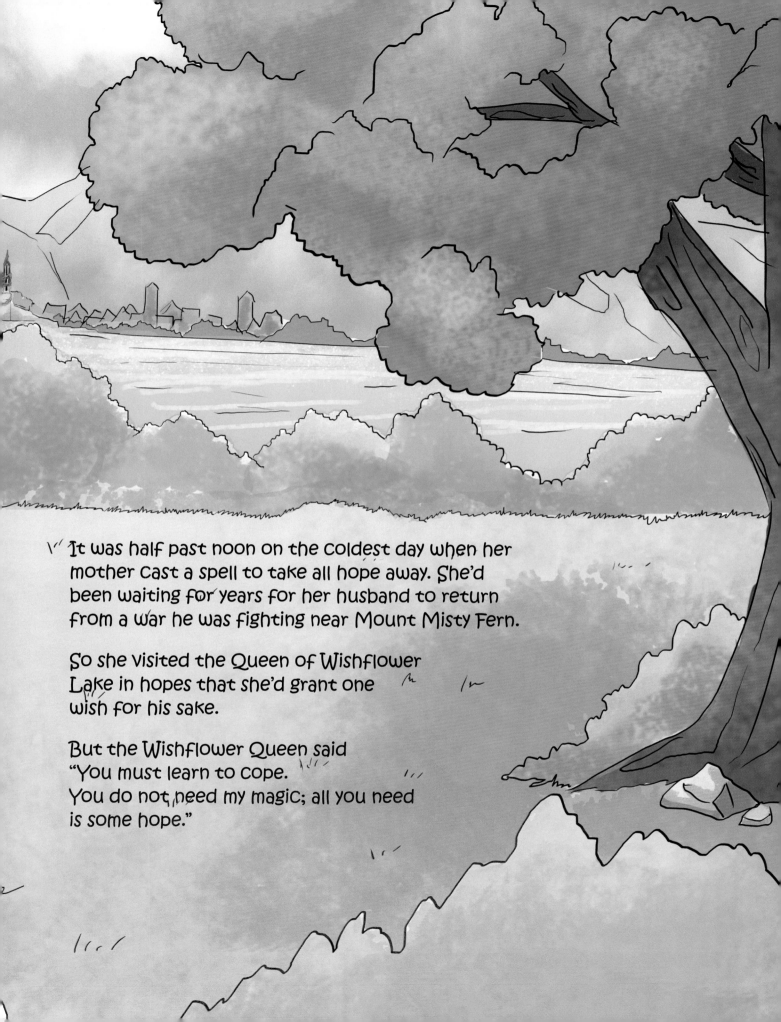

It was half past noon on the coldest day when her
mother cast a spell to take all hope away. She'd
been waiting for years for her husband to return
from a war he was fighting near Mount Misty Fern.

So she visited the Queen of Wishflower
Lake in hopes that she'd grant one
wish for his sake.

But the Wishflower Queen said
"You must learn to cope.
You do not need my magic; all you need
is some hope."

Kayla's mother was upset when she didn't get her way, so she cast out a spell on the kingdom that day.
She had visited a sorcerer with a powerful potion to spread doubt and fear from ocean to ocean.

Across Bubble Bridge to the caves of Owl Mountain, the sorcerer conjured his spell from a fountain.

"Thy Wishflower Princess will no longer spread hope and the rest of the world will now learn how to cope."

As the new sun rose, evil cast its net, upon Wishflower Lake where the young princess slept.

Waking up to the fields where hope once bloomed the Wishflower Princess felt hopeless and doomed.

One by one, she kept sneezing away all the wishflower petals before she could say...

"Lotus brutis hicum scope grant this wish for those with hope." But without her magical words to assist, the powerful flowers were nothing but mist.

"I know what to do," said Sir Chris with a notion, "I heard of a witch with a powerful potion. She can change a spell from bad to good; she's The Witch of Eternity from Wonderland Woods."

So they left to find her before it was too late, to save the kingdom from a horrible fate. As darkness fell they came upon troubles, a treacherous bridge made from nothing but bubbles.

"This must be the place, Kayla said with a mutter, I'm cold and scared, and I'm starting to shutter."

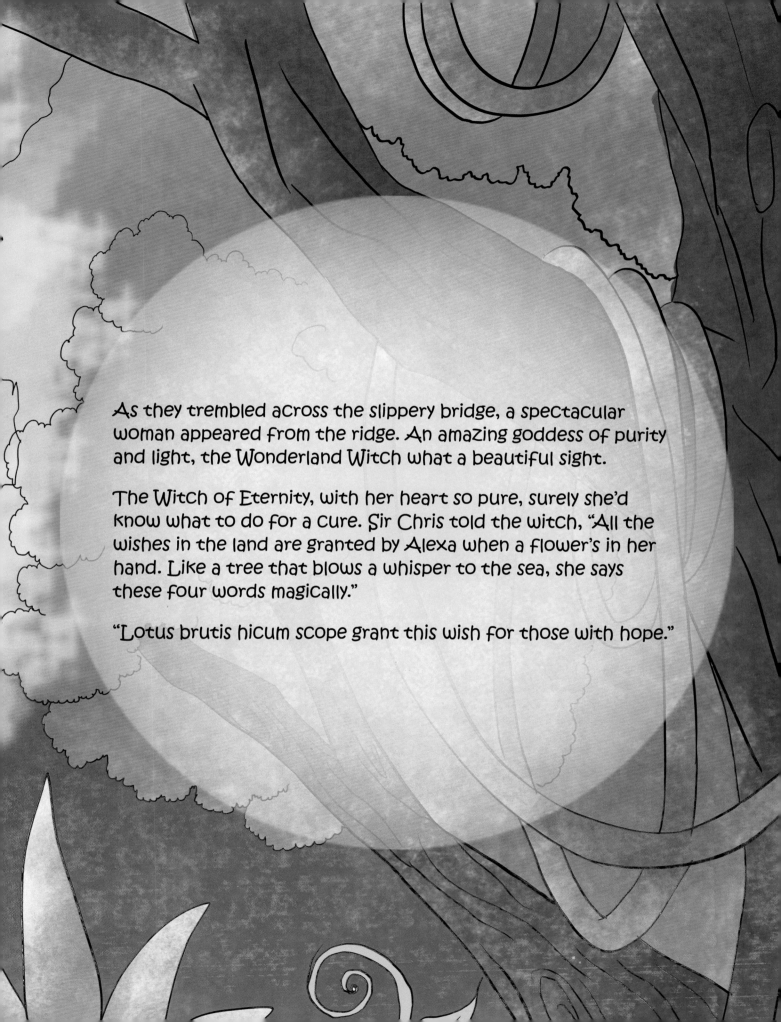

As they trembled across the slippery bridge, a spectacular woman appeared from the ridge. An amazing goddess of purity and light, the Wonderland Witch what a beautiful sight.

The Witch of Eternity, with her heart so pure, surely she'd know what to do for a cure. Sir Chris told the witch, "All the wishes in the land are granted by Alexa when a flower's in her hand. Like a tree that blows a whisper to the sea, she says these four words magically."

"Lotus brutis hicum scope grant this wish for those with hope."

"Please understand she's
no ordinary girl, she' part tree
and part flower with the soul
of a pearl.

Purity of kindness is her magical
power; it comes from the nature that
lives in her flower. She's Mother Nature's
child with the world in her care, pollinating life
with the bees from her hair."

"She protects the world's climate and feeds the world hope, creating something new from something once broke. But now that she's stricken with a terrible spell, the people of our planet aren't doing very well. Sadly the kingdom has filled up with doubt since Princess Alexa started sneezing hope out."

A flickering light danced in the sky as the Witch of Eternity, slowly passed by. "I know who you are, and from what you have told me it sounds like the potion is standing before me."

"You see it's very simple," said the all-knowing Witch, "its hope that will cure this princess's twitch. The most doubtful person in all of the land must wish on a flower and believe again."

"We must find my mother," Lady Kayla said in haste, "we have to go now, there's no time to waste."

So they thanked the witch and hurried to town where they found her mother with a sorrowful frown.

"Mother," Lady Kayla said, "you must try to believe that father will return with his heart on his sleeve."

"I'll try for you," said her mother with a smile, "I'll go to the forest and pray for a while."

They watched as she wandered far into the trees and held up a wishflower as she knelt to her knees.

She closed her eyes and blew it a kiss and watched as the wishflower broke into mist.

"Though time has passed and hopes turned to despair, I believe that my wishflower is still in the air."

The soft sprays of snow now drifted with ease, gently falling nearby to stems in the trees.

Yet one small speck kept flying up high, it held up her dreams as it floated on by...

That small speck drifted till it landed with grace, on the nose of the beautiful princess's face.

But Princess Alexa didn't sneeze, sniff or swish instead what she did was grant her a wish.

Lotus brutis hicum scope grant this wish for those with hope."

The next day all hope was restored to the land because Lady Kayla's mother believed again.

On the very next day, Kayla's father appeared, just as they'd hope for, for years and years.

And as for Princess Alexa, well she never sneezed again...

At least not on a wishflower filled
with hope! - The End

Note from the author: Help Princess Alexa by planting your own HOPE and save our beautiful planet. Wishflowers are dandelions that grow wild throughout the world. "Wildings" are being devastated through continued use of weed killers and other chemicals that are leaching into the atmosphere. Unfortunately the wishflower (dandelions), like many other wild flowers are considered weeds, and are being destroyed at an alarming rate. Please plant more "wildings" and help the bees pollinate the planet. Pollination is what helps plants grow and produces most of our food. When bees transfer pollen between flowers and plants, they keep the cycle of life turning. You can help save Earth and plant HOPE for future generations. I have included links to a few of my favorite online seed stores where you can get packets of wildflower mixtures of all kinds and help save the bee pollination and our planet.

www.myseedneeds.com

www.bulkwildflowers.com

www.groworganic.com

Printed in the United States
By Bookmasters